MAX AND
ADVENTURE IN
WARTIME BRITAIN!

BY SAMANTHA METCALF

ILLUSTRATED BY IAN R. WARD

Second edition
Published in Great Britain in 2020 by:
Mysteries in Time Limited
info@mysteriesintime.co.uk

This book is a work of fiction and, except in the case of historical fact,
any resemblance to actual persons, living or dead, is purely coincidental.

Illustrated by Ian R. Ward
www.ianrward.co.uk

A catalogue record for this book is available from the British Library.

ISBN 978-0-9935660-2-8

Hi! I'm Katie and I am 8 years old. Max is my older brother. He's really clever. He helps me with my home work when I'm stuck. He knows everything! But don't tell him I said that. He can get really annoying and know-it-all. He is always telling me stuff, but sometimes it's just too much. All I want is a simple answer, like 'yes' or 'no'. Instead, it's always 'maybe, because...' So annoying.

But he's not so bad. He always looks out for me. And we have fun playing games together.

I think my favourite thing is playing outside in any weather! I love going to the park, especially the adventure playground with the huge, curly slide. You can go really fast on that one, especially when you lie down! Mum hates it when I come home covered in mud, but I can't help it. The fun parts of the park are always the muddiest.

Hey, I'm Max and I'm 11. I love reading. I read comics and cartoons that make me laugh, and I read adventure stories about knights and castles, or pirates and buried treasure! Mum is always telling me I have an over-active imagination. I can't help it. My mind just starts picturing loads of weird stuff.

I also love solving puzzles. Grandpa always buys me books full of word-searches and crosswords. I like to time myself and see how fast I can solve them.

Katie is my younger sister. She is really energetic and fun to be around. She's really fast and sporty. I wish I could be as good as her at sports. But don't tell her I said that. She can also be really annoying, when she can't sit still for more than five minutes. And she doesn't stop talking!

But she's cool. I'm pleased she's my sister.

1

It was Saturday. Max and Katie were at their favourite park, the one with the really wide slide. It was wide enough that Max and Katie could slide down at the same time, side-by-side. They did what all brothers and sisters would do: they had a race.

They got into position at the top, arms on the metal handles. Ready.

Max counted backwards from three loudly, then they both launched themselves forward with as much power as they could. Max went faster, but his legs and arms flew in all directions as he went over the bump in the middle.

Max landed face down in a muddy puddle at the bottom. Katie landed sitting upright a few seconds after him. She landed with a splash, covering Max with a fresh wave of mud.

They giggled the whole way home.

Back home, they were about to flop onto the soft, over-sized cushions of the sofa, when Mum's high-pitched shriek stopped them in their tracks.

"STOP! You're both COVERED in mud!" she yelled with her hands on her face in horror. "Do NOT sit there until you're clean!" She now had one hand on her hip, the other was pointing up the stairs. "Get changed NOW!"

Max and Katie winced at the sharp tone of

their mother's angry voice. "Sorry, Mum," they said together as they stepped past her.

Max knew Mum felt guilty for shouting, because she quickly called after them in a softer voice.

"The postman came while you were out. Get changed quickly and you can have your parcel."

Max fist-pumped the air. It was time for another adventure.

They got changed at lightning speed. Katie was especially fast; her jumper was not only inside-out, but back-to-front as well. Max didn't have time to tell her. He was too excited.

Max and Katie collected the turquoise parcel from Mum and bounced back up the stairs. When they were safely away from Mum's attention, they opened the box.

Max found the Mission Plan and read it out loud for Katie.

Mission Plan

Place: Wales
Date: October 1940

During the Second World War, thousands of children were evacuated from Britain's cities, coastal towns and industrial areas. It wasn't safe for them any more with enemy aeroplanes bombing each night.

A small group of children were evacuated from the city and sent to an old man's farm house in the Welsh countryside. At first, everything was fine. But when things started to go missing, he blamed the children in his house. However, the items were not things a child would want to take.

The mystery was never solved. The owner, Mr Jones, stopped trusting people. He fired all his staff. He sent away all the children and never let another child enter his home ever again. His home became cold and neglected, the gardens were overgrown, and he never looked after himself. He spent the rest of his days living a lonely life.

Task:

1. Find some suitable clothes and travel back to 1940.
2. Find out who was stealing from Mr Jones and why.

Good luck.

2

Katie sniffed loudly and rubbed her nose on her sleeve. "That's so sad," she sobbed. "We have to help him."

Max pulled out the history book to learn about World War Two. They read about children getting evacuated from towns and being sent to live with strangers in the countryside. They read about people blacking out their windows at night. They read about air raid shelters, sirens and gas masks. They found out who the Nazis were. Katie was upset for a second time when she learnt about the Holocaust.

"It's just horrible," she sniffed. "How could people treat other people like that?"

Max agreed. Even *he* had a tear in his eye. He decided to cheer themselves up by going to find some 1940s clothes. "Let's go visit Grandpa."

Max put the history book back inside the box

and hid it deep underneath his bed, while Katie turned her jumper the right way round. They then headed downstairs. "Remember, act normal," warned Max.

Katie nodded, and they went downstairs. Max noticed Katie wasn't walking, she was sauntering. Max nudged her and whispered to her. "What are you doing?! Walk normally!"

"I am!" she hissed back. "This is my I'm-not-doing-anything-unusual walk."

Luckily, Mum was in the lounge reading a book in her favourite seat, so she didn't notice Katie's unnatural natural walk.

In fact, when Max told her where they were going, she didn't even look up. She just waved her hand.

"OK dear. Look after your sister."

That was easy. Now for Grandpa.

3

When they got to their grandfather's fancy dress shop, they asked him if he would like to take a break.

"We'll look after the shop. You work too hard," they insisted. "Go and make yourself a cup of tea."

Grandpa smiled, thanked them and went into a back room. Now was their chance. They quickly found the rail of clothes from the 1940s and picked out some simple clothes.

"Quick!" hissed Max. "Grandpa will be back any minute now!"

They quickly filled a bag with their clothes before their grandfather returned with his cup of tea. When Grandpa offered them a chocolate biscuit to say thank you for being so thoughtful, Max suddenly felt too guilty about lying to accept one. Katie didn't. She even took Max's share and wolfed it down happily in no time.

4

Back in Max's bedroom, they got changed into their 1940s clothes. Katie thought Max looked funny in his long shorts. Katie had a grey skirt just below her knee and a blue cardigan. They also had hats and coats. They checked themselves in the mirror and adjusted their hats. When they were happy with their appearance, Max pulled out their parcel and emptied the contents on the floor.

Inside, they found a brown label. One side they could write their name and address on, the other already said: Mr Jones, Farmhouse Cottage, New Vale, Wales. Max checked the instructions. "The mini Time Travel Computer is hidden inside a label this time, instead of a sticker," he read out loud.

They threaded the string through the top button hole of their jackets and tied the label in place with a knot, just like the evacuees in the photos.

They each had a brown box with a string handle.

"What's this?" asked Katie.

"That's a gas mask," explained Max. "All evacuees had to carry one everywhere, in case of an attack."

But Katie was only half-listening. She was more interested in the ration book. "What was rationing?"

"There was a shortage of even simple foods, like eggs, milk, butter and sugar," explained Max. "So people were rationed. That means they were only allowed to buy a set amount of these things each week."

"Eggs, milk and sugar? That's fine," decided Katie.

"At least chocolate was OK. I couldn't live without chocolate or ice-cream."

Max threw his hands in the air. "Chocolate WAS rationed!" he exclaimed. "Ice-cream wasn't very easy to get either, since it's made from EGGS, MILK and SUGAR!"

Katie looked horrified. "Oh. Well, let's solve this mystery as quickly as we can. The 1940s sound awful."

Before Katie could ask any more questions, Max pressed the large red button on the time machine. "Here we go again!"

The safe, familiar walls of Max's bedroom disappeared and colours began to spin around them. Max was getting dizzy, so he closed his eyes.

When he felt solid ground beneath his feet again, he opened his eyes and looked around.

5

They were on a noisy train station platform. The train that was arriving was puffing clouds of smoke from a tall chimney at the front of the engine.

Everyone covered their mouths and noses with their sleeves as the platform was engulfed in smoke.

Katie's ears hurt with the high shriek from the train's brakes as it came to a stop. "Aaaah!" she yelled as she put her fingers in her ears. "It's even more screechy than Mum's singing!"

An important-looking man in a uniform checked Max and Katie's labels and led them past sobbing mothers onto the waiting steam train. Soon, dozens of other children piled into their carriage. Max and Katie squeezed up to the window to make space.

The station master blew his whistle; the train was ready to leave. There was a whoosh of steam. The train juddered forwards, then let out a loud whistle.

The mums running alongside the departing train couldn't keep up and stood watching as their children were carried away to an unknown safety.

There were mixed feelings on the train. Many children were crying. They didn't know when they would see their families again. But some were excited.

"Don't worry," an older boy told everyone. "It's an adventure!"

Max smiled. They knew all about adventures.

6

The journey seemed like it would go on forever. Everyone was tired, hungry and thirsty.

After four hours, the train stopped at a tiny station with a very short platform surrounded by fields. Max and Katie heard their names called out and they waved goodbye to their new friends on the train. "Oi, Max," called the boy who had been sitting next to him. "Be on the look-out! There's a missing German somewhere round here!" Max didn't have time to ask him what he meant, because he was dragged off the train by Katie. "Come on, Max!" she huffed and puffed. "We have to get off NOW!"

They jumped down onto the platform. The station master checked their labels against his list.

"Max and Katie, you are going to stay at the old farmhouse," he said. "This is Betty."

A friendly lady with fiery red hair and wearing a

brown coat gave them a big smile and a hug. "Nice to meet you both," she said. "We have space for two more evacuees, so we will just choose them and then get back to the farm."

They walked to the village hall, where dozens of children were waiting to be picked.

Max and Katie watched the terrible scene play out in front of them. Local people arrived and walked up and down the line. They judged the children, asking them to turn around.

Betty tutted to herself. "They're not animals at the market," she said in disgust. "They're children!"

Katie noticed that the girls with curly hair got picked first. Max saw that the tall, stronger boys also got picked first. "It's like PE all over again," he said. "I'm always the last to get picked. It's a horrible feeling."

There was suddenly a loud cry from a little boy with chubby cheeks. He was clinging to an older girl, who had been picked by an old couple.

"Mum said we have to stick together," announced the girl. "If you take me, you have to take my brother too." The boy clung to his sister.

The old couple didn't look happy about this. Their wrinkled faces frowned even more. "But he's too young to help us in the shop!"

Just as the boy's bottom lip started to wobble, Betty stepped in. "Oh, don't worry dear, I can take two. Why don't you both come with me?" She bent down and gave the little boy a warm cuddle.

Katie saw the boy wipe his snotty nose on Betty's shoulder.

"Let's go," said Betty, leading the four of them outside, where a man was waiting with a horse and cart.

7

They were all lifted up onto the cart by the driver, who introduced himself as George. They got comfortable as they sat on bundles of hay. The two other children introduced themselves as Jack and Harriet. Harriet's two plaits were tied with red ribbon. Jack had a round face with rosy red cheeks.

"I'm ten, Jack's five," said Harriet.

The powerful horse pulled them along quiet country lanes. They giggled and pinched their noses against the smell of manure. Except for the clatter of hooves against stones and the cart's wheels, the only sounds they could hear were the leaves in the breeze and the distant sound of a train's whistle.

They drove up to a large square house with a tall chimney that was puffing thick smoke into the air.

"Wow!" exclaimed Katie. "This place is huge! We'll get lost!"

"And look – we're by the seaside!" shrieked Jack. "I've never been to the seaside before."

"Jack, you've never even left the city before!" laughed Harriet.

Jack was lifted down by the driver. Max and Harriet jumped down from the cart themselves. Katie did the same, but she fell over as she landed. They all laughed together.

This did feel like a holiday after all!

8

There were three people waiting to greet them at the door. Betty introduced them all, one by one.

"Well, you've already met George," she said, patting his shoulder. "He's the village mechanic. He also looks after our horses and drives the cart."

"Very pleased to meet you all," he said.

Betty moved along. "This is Mr Lang, our new gardener. He only arrived three weeks ago, but he has already settled in very well." Mr Lang gave an awkward wave to everyone. Betty continued, "Don't expect a conversation. He's a man of few words."

She turned to the last person there, an old man with a kind smile. "And this is Farmer Eddie."

He lifted his flat cap and smiled. "Come find me tomorrow and I might even let you feed the animals!" he said.

Betty smiled, then shivered as a gust of wind

swirled around them. "Come on, let's get inside before we blow away!"

Inside, Betty hung their hats, coats and gas mask boxes up on a coat-stand. "I'm the housekeeper, so if there's anything you need, just ask me." she said. Betty checked the time on the tall grandfather clock. "Come on, it's not too late. I'll take you to meet Mr Jones, the owner of this farm!"

Betty led them up the creaking stairs. She stopped in the hallway and fussed over their appearances. She licked her thumb and rubbed at a smudge on Jack's cheek. She smoothed Katie's hair and pulled Max's hands out of his pockets.

The door was slightly ajar. Max could see a noticeboard with newspaper cuttings pinned up messily, some overlapping others. He squinted to read the headlines. He could make out a few words... "German Pilot Missing... Aeroplane... shot down... dangerous... Wales."

9

Betty knocked on the door and listened closely.

"Come in," they heard from inside.

Betty opened the door and ushered them in, introducing them one by one.

Mr Jones was an old man with lots of lines on his face. He had kind eyes and smiled at the four children. "Very pleased to meet you all," he said. "You are all very welcome. Now, any questions?"

Jack's arm shot in the air.

Mr Jones peered down at him. "Yes?"

"Can we - are we – may we…" Jack was struggling to find the right words in his excitement. "Can we go exploring?" Jack's eyes were alive and his cheeks were even more rosy than normal.

Mr Jones laughed. "Yes! You may explore the house and the gardens. I just have a couple of rules."

Katie almost groaned, but stopped herself in

time. She hated rules. Rules stopped fun.

"Don't go too close to those cliffs," he pointed out through the large window towards the sea. "A large gust of wind may just carry you over the edge. And be careful with the animals. Cows and horses are large beasts with hard hooves. They could do a lot of damage to a little person, such as yourselves."

They thanked Mr Jones and left him in peace. Max was the last person through the door, and he heard Mr Jones ask Betty an interesting question.

"Have you seen my torch, Betty? I can't find it anywhere."

10

"Follow me," said Betty. "You must all be very hungry after that long journey." She led them into a large kitchen and gave them each a bowl of delicious vegetable broth. Katie was so hungry that she ate too quickly. Max rolled his eyes when she moaned that she had burnt her mouth.

After dinner, Jack yawned noisily.

Betty smiled. "Come on, I'll take you to your room."

They picked up their small suitcases and followed Betty in silence up the wooden stairs to their room.

There were four wooden beds in a row, lined up along the wall opposite the windows.

It was getting dark, so Betty lit two gas lamps then quickly pulled the thick black curtains closed across the two large windows. She smoothed them, until there was no chance of any light escaping.

"Now I don't have many rules," said Betty. "But you all know by now that you must never open these curtains when the lamp is on. We don't want Jerry seeing where we are, do we?"

They all shook their heads. Katie waited until Betty had gone before whispering to Max. "Who's Jerry, and why do we have to hide from him?"

Max smiled. "Jerry's not a person. It's what people called the Germans during the war."

"Oh. But why would our curtains being open upset them so much?"

"It was for safety. From September 1940 there were night-time bombing raids over Britain's cities. That's why children were evacuated. If enemy planes spotted lights below, then they could use it as a target. So everyone blacked out their windows at night to keep them safe."

Katie double-checked that the curtains were shut. She didn't want to get spotted by an enemy plane!

11

Max finally dozed off. He dreamt that he'd left the black-out curtain open and hundreds of planes flew overhead. He pictured the light shining up into the sky like a beacon, announcing where they were.

He woke with a start from his nightmare and sat up. He listened for planes, but all was peaceful, all except for the bone-rattling sound of Jack snoring.

The gas lamp was turned off, so the room was dark. Even so, Max wanted to check the window was covered. In the pitch black, he got up. He felt his way along the wall until he reached the window.

He checked the curtain. Closed. They were safe.

"Well," thought Max, "there's no light in the room, so what's the harm in looking out?"

Max carefully lifted the black-out curtain and checked the sky for planes. All clear. The moon was full and bright. Everything was quiet and still.

Max was about to go back to bed, when something caught his eye outside. Something had moved out there. Max looked closer, allowing his eyes to adjust to the dark. Just when he thought he must have imagined it, he saw it again.

What was it? It was too slow for a bat or an owl. It was too large for a fox. He watched patiently for several minutes before he saw it again.

It wasn't something.

It was someone.

Someone was creeping around in the shadows. Max saw the figure tiptoe towards the cliffs, where it stopped. There was such a long gap between sightings that Max began to think that it must all be in his imagination.

But then he saw a flash of light. Sometimes just a short flash, sometimes longer. It was faint and hard to see. But it was definitely a series of flashes.

Max kept checking the room nervously, convinced his heart was beating so loudly that it would wake everyone else up.

Max watched the scene outside for a long time. He eventually fell asleep leaning against the window sill, propping his chin on his hand. He woke with a start when gravity took over and his knee wobbled.

By now, the horizon was starting to gain a warm glow as the sun began to rise over the hills. Max scanned the gardens below, but all was now still. He tiptoed back to bed and quickly fell into a deep sleep.

12

"Wake up!" he heard. "Max, wake up!"

Max wiped his sweaty forehead and sat up in bed.

"Are you OK?" asked Katie. "You were shouting in your sleep!"

"Oh, yes, fine," said Max. "What time is it?" He squinted at the window. The curtains were pulled back and the sun was streaming into the dusty attic room. The glass panes had white tape criss-crossing from corner to corner. Max's tired eyes saw a pattern of diamonds as the panes blurred together.

"It's breakfast time!" replied Katie. "We've been up for ages. I don't know why you're being so lazy."

Just then, Max remembered what he had seen in the garden. He wanted to tell Katie, but he decided to save it for later, when they could talk in private.

Max got up and got dressed, then they went downstairs to the kitchen, where Betty was busy stoking the fire in the large stove. They had home-made bread with butter, boiled eggs and even a rasher of bacon for breakfast.

"What happened to rationing?" asked Katie.

"I know!" said Harriet happily, spraying crumbs everywhere. "There are lots of eggs and lots of milk here in the countryside. It's so much better than the food we get in the city!"

After breakfast, Max and Katie followed Harriet and Jack outside to go exploring. The sun was hiding behind the clouds, but they didn't notice how cold it was.

They ran everywhere, from the cow sheds to the fields, where they watched five horses galloping and shaking their manes as they came to a stop. They found a pond. Jack chased the ducks, until two very large, very angry swans chased Jack in revenge.

They all giggled as they explored. They eventually collapsed under a large oak tree at the edge of a forest for a rest. Once they had caught their breath, Jack jumped up.

"Let's explore the forest!" he suggested. Harriet agreed and stood up.

Katie got up too, but Max stopped her.

"Katie, I'm afraid we can't go. We promised Mum we would write to her straight away, remember?"

Katie frowned as she watched her new friends skip off for more fun.

"Why do you have to be such a spoil-sport?"

"Er, we're here on a mission!" replied Max. "Did you hear Mr Jones earlier? His torch is missing."

Max told Katie what he had seen in the night. "It must be connected. Whoever stole his torch was outside last night."

"But why?" asked Katie. "What were they doing?"

"Good question."

Max and Katie agreed to split up to see what they could find out.

13

Just outside, Katie could hear someone singing and went to investigate. She met Farmer Eddie.

"Hello," he said, standing up tall with his hands on his hips. "Have you settled in? I imagine life here is quite different to what you're used to in the city. Not a lot happens out here. Very peaceful."

Katie nodded. "What are you doing? Can I help?"

Farmer Eddie looked pleased with the offer. "Yes! You could help me feed the cows. Grab that bucket over there," he said, pointing. "Follow me."

Farmer Eddie marched off down the path, away from the house. It wasn't long before they reached the cow shed. Eddie showed Katie how to spread the feed around. Katie was enjoying herself, watching the funny way cows eat their food. She tried to copy the way their mouths moved round and round in circles as they ate.

Farmer Eddie stopped suddenly and dropped his bucket. "What the..?"

Something had caught his attention. Eddie was peering into the corner of the cow shed, where there was a dark stain on the ground.

"What is it?" asked Katie.

Farmer Eddie looked at Katie. His expression was very serious and his face was suddenly very pale.

"Something or someone must have hurt themselves," he replied quietly. "I think it's blood."

14

Meanwhile, Max was exploring the gardens. He followed the sound of metal on metal and found himself at the open door to a large garage. There was an old motorbike there with a large light at the front.

"Hello?" he called out.

A head popped up from behind the bike. "Oh, hello young man," said the driver from yesterday.

"What are you doing?" asked Max.

"I'm fixing this old motorbike," said George. "Would you pass me that spanner over there?"

Max moved closer, reached for the spanner and passed it over. The motorbike was different to modern bikes. There was no plastic, just metal.

"Is it nearly finished?" asked Max.

"It should run alright," said George, "but there's a long way to go before she looks shiny again."

Max decided to find out a little more about Mr

Jones. "Er, Mr Jones seems really friendly," he said.

"Yes, he is," he replied. "He's a wise man with a lot of interesting stories to tell. He used to work as a code breaker, you know, in the Great War. But he is very quiet at the moment. He is distracted by that missing pilot." George's voice trailed off. He was trying to tighten some bolts with the spanner, but he was struggling to see. "Can you see my glasses lying anywhere?" he asked Max. "I haven't seen them all day and I'm as blind as a bat without them."

Max searched everywhere, from the workbenches to the cupboards. He even looked inside the toolbox by the door, but no sign of the glasses.

"First my tools start going missing, now my glasses!" said George, shaking his head. "They must be here somewhere!"

Was this another mysteriously disappearing object, or just something misplaced by a forgetful old man?

15

Katie wandered around to the back of the house. She was on her way inside, when she overheard someone whistling. She followed the sound and found the gardener planting seeds in a flowerbed.

"Hi," said Katie happily. Mr Lang jumped. "Oh, sorry Mr Lang, I didn't mean to scare you!"

He waved his hand and smiled at Katie, but it felt forced. Cold. Katie felt like she was in the way.

She chose to ignore the feeling. Max was always saying she was good at ignoring people's feelings.

"Er, nice weather today," she said hopefully. Mr Lang acted like he hadn't heard and carried on digging. Katie took a deep breath and puffed out her cheeks trying to think of something to say. This was a strange feeling: she had nothing to say. She realised this was the first time she'd ever been speechless!

"I can't wait until I see my brother and tell him

I'm speechless!" said Katie out loud. "He won't believe me. He always calls me a chatterbox. Or a bigmouth. Or a blabbermouth. But I don't think that's fair. Just because I have a lot to say doesn't mean he should call me names." Katie realised that Mr Lang had stopped and was looking at her, frowning. He looked confused. Or annoyed. Katie thought maybe he was hard of hearing, like Grandpa, but decided to leave quickly. She shivered.

He really didn't want her there.

16

Max strolled up to the house and opened the front door. There was a pile of letters on the doormat. He picked them up just as Betty walked past.

"Oh, I forgot all about the post today! Would you please take those letters up to Mr Jones? I'm rushed off my feet now I have four extra mouths to feed!"

Betty smiled and went into the kitchen.

The stairs creaked once more under Max's feet. He reached the first floor and he could see Mr Jones' door was slightly ajar. He tiptoed closer.

"Don't be shy," came a voice from inside.

Max wanted to run away, but instead he pushed the door open and stepped inside. Mr Jones put his newspaper down and turned to look at Max.

"Have you settled in well, young Max?" he asked, taking his glasses off the end of his nose.

Max nodded. "Yes, thank you," he said. "Sorry, I

didn't mean to interrupt your work."

"No bother," said Mr Jones kindly. "I've been reading for so long today that I think I'm going cross-eyed!"

Max held out his hand with the letters.

"Oh yes, thank you, Max." Mr Jones flicked through the letters and found a photograph mixed in. "Oh, that's not post. It must belong to Betty or someone else. You had better give it back. I know many things are going missing around here at the moment, let's not add this to the list!"

Max looked at Mr Jones' desk as he took back the picture. "What are you working on?" he asked.

"Well, I like to study the local papers and listen to the wireless, looking for anything strange. I used to be in the army, you see. I served in the First World War as a code breaker. It's very interesting work when you get a break-through. The rest of the time it can be rather dull."

"What did you have to do?" asked Max.

"I studied patterns. I listened out for messages in Morse code. I looked for strange announcements in newspapers." Mr Jones took a deep breath in and sighed loudly. "I haven't found anything unusual. Well, I might have done, except someone has taken my wireless so I haven't heard any news for days!"

"What's Morse code?" asked Max.

"It's very clever, but very simple," explained Mr Jones. "Each letter of the alphabet is represented by either dots or dashes, or a mixture of dots and dashes. It's a code. You can communicate using sounds or flashes of light."

Max didn't hear much of what Mr Jones said after that. He was too busy thinking about Morse code. Could that be what those flashes of light were last night? Had someone stolen Mr Jones' torch to send a message to someone using Morse code?

Max realised Mr Jones was staring straight at him with a frown. "Have you seen it?" he asked. "Have you seen my wireless?"

Max suddenly felt uncomfortable, and stood up. "Er, no, no I h-h-haven't," he stammered. "Excuse m-m-me." Max backed out of the room, bumping into the door frame as he went, then raced down the hallway and down the stairs so quickly, he didn't even notice that Mr Jones was standing at the doorway, watching him.

17

Max went straight to the kitchen and gave the photograph to Betty, explaining what Mr Jones had said. She looked confused, but took the photograph with a worried expression.

Max didn't linger. He needed some air. He burst through the front door just as Katie was running up the driveway.

Max told Katie all about Mr Jones' missing wireless.

"Wireless?" asked Katie loudly. "They didn't even have the internet *with* wires in the 1940s, how could they have wireless?!"

"People in the 1940s called the radio 'the wireless'," explained Max. "Mr Jones has lost his radio."

Katie told Max all about the blood stain in the cow shed. "Someone must have been hurt badly."

Max realised what must have happened. "The key to the mystery is with this missing German pilot," he explained.

"When did the pilot disappear?" asked Katie.

"It was 17th September 1940, just over three weeks ago." Max stopped and looked at Katie with his hands on his head. "Of course! Three weeks ago!"

"Three weeks ago? Why is that important?"

"Three weeks ago!" exclaimed Max.

"Yes, Max, I get it. Something happened three weeks ago." Katie's hands were on her hips and she was frowning at her annoying brother. "What happened and why is it important?"

Max looked at his sister. "Mr Lang started working here three weeks ago."

18

"Let me get this straight," said Katie. "You think Mr Lang the gardener is the missing German pilot?"

Max nodded enthusiastically. "Well, you met him earlier, what do you think?"

Katie thought back to her very odd, very one-sided conversation with Mr Lang. "Well, come to think of it," she said slowly, "he didn't say anything. In fact, he looked like he didn't understand a word I said!"

Max remembered the strange photograph that was mixed in with the letters. He thought back to what Mr Jones had said about codes and secret messages.

"The photograph!" he shouted, throwing his hands on his head. "Of course!"

Max turned abruptly and ran back into the house. Katie threw her hands in the air. "I guess I'll just follow you, shall I?"

Katie found Max in the hallway, holding a photograph and peering at it closely.

There were heavy footsteps on the stairs. Mr Jones appeared. He looked even angrier than before.

"What are you children doing snooping around in here? Looking for something else to steal? Hmmm?"

Max knew he had to be brave. He held out the photograph. "I know there have been lots of things going missing here, but I promise you we are not to blame. We're trying to help you. We think Mr Lang is the missing German pilot from your newspaper report." Max's mouth was dry. "I think this photograph is the key to the whole mystery."

Max stood still, holding out the photograph. Mr Jones was silent. He was watching Max closely. Max started to feel uncomfortable.

19

Max cleared his throat and continued. "This photograph was delivered with the post this morning. I think there might be a code in the picture, or a secret message on the back…"

Mr Jones was now staring at the photograph in Max's outstretched hand. He nodded slightly, then took the photograph from Max's now aching hand. Mr Jones put his glasses on the end of his nose and peered through the thick glass at the picture.

"Yes, yes," he said quietly, almost to himself. He turned it over and held the blank side close to his eyes, turning it in the light. "Yes!" he said, this time more confidently. He moved to the table lamp and tilted the photograph against the lamp.

"What is he doing?" whispered Katie. "Has he gone mad?" Max hissed for her to be quiet. She clearly thought Mr Jones must be hard of hearing.

He wasn't.

"Well, dear Katie, I have not gone mad," he replied, not once taking his eyes off the picture. "Your brother is very clever. He spotted something even I, a professional code-breaker, missed."

Katie rolled her eyes. "Alright, alright. What did Mr Clever Clogs spot?" she asked.

"There is a secret message written on the back of this picture. It's written in lemon juice, which is invisible until the paper is warmed up on something hot like a light-bulb." Mr Jones waved them over.

Katie stepped closer and saw a message appearing out of nowhere. "What does it say?" she asked.

"It's in German. It's a secret message to the missing pilot." Mr Jones was suddenly very anxious. "Who else saw this photograph? Think carefully."

Max scratched his head. "Er, well I picked up the post myself, then Betty asked me to bring it all straight to you," he said slowly. "Then you gave me the photograph back and I left it on this table." Max thought some more. "The only other person in this part of the house in the last five minutes is... is..."

"Yes?" prompted Mr Jones.

"Is Betty. I heard her singing in the kitchen." Max felt like he was telling tales and didn't like it.

Mr Jones quickly stuck his head into the kitchen and called out Betty's name. There was no answer. "Quick, there is no time to lose," he said. "We must find Betty before something happens to her. She could be in terrible danger."

20

They all raced outside and along the path. They first saw Farmer Eddie.

"Eddie, have you seen Betty? It is very important," urged Mr Jones.

"Oh, yes sir, she went that way, less than five minutes ago," he replied, pointing down the lane towards the cliffs.

They all set off in the direction of the sea. They ran past Jack and Harriet, who were climbing a tree and giggling. They jumped down and chased after them, curious about what could have brought the master of the house running outside in his slippers.

They reached the edge of the cliff, where there were some steep, uneven stone steps down the face of the cliff. They couldn't see much of the beach from here, because large rocks jutted out towards the sea.

Mr Jones told them to be careful as they went

down. "Hold the rail and watch your step. It's a long way down if you fall."

They were all silent as they climbed down. First was Mr Jones, then Max and Katie, and finally Jack and Harriet. Jack was a lot slower with his little legs, and Harriet stayed with him.

At the bottom, they shielded their eyes from the sun as they scanned the beach for people. They could see two people there. One of them was definitely Betty. The sun was shining off her red hair.

"Who is she with?" asked Katie. "Has Mr Lang taken her hostage?"

21

Both Betty and her mystery companion were facing out to sea, so Mr Jones, Max and Katie were able to creep up without being spotted. The waves crashing onto the shore covered any sound they made. As they got much closer, Mr Jones held up his hand, signalling them to stop.

Mr Jones spoke slowly and carefully. "Please don't be alarmed, we're not here to hurt you." Betty and the young man spun round, shocked.

It wasn't Mr Lang.

"Betty, has this man hurt you in any way?"

Betty looked from Mr Jones to the young man and back. "Hurt? No! How could...? Look at him!"

They all looked at this man next to her. His left arm was held in a sling across his chest and he had bandages wrapped around his head, covering his right eye. Max understood Betty's surprise. There was no way this man could hurt anyone in that state!

By now, Jack and Harriet had joined them.

Katie was confused. "So is this the German pilot who went missing from the crashed plane?"

Jack and Harriet gasped in shock. Jack stepped back in horror. He stumbled in the sand and fell. Harriet helped him up, holding his hand tightly.

"Yes, this is the German pilot, but you must hear the full story before you judge him. Or me."

Mr Jones nodded. "Go ahead."

"Well, it all started nearly three weeks ago," started Betty. "I was out collecting some milk from the cows, when I saw a trail of dark spots leading from the cow shed. They led out towards the edge of the cliff. I followed, thinking that maybe there was a hurt animal." Betty paused, looked at everyone, then continued. "I reached the edge of the cliff, but couldn't see anything. Then I heard a noise behind me. I turned quickly, but lost my footing and slipped."

"The ground disappeared from beneath me, my bucket crashed down to the beach below. I was clinging on for dear life. I screamed for help, but the wind was howling and throwing my voice back out to sea. I thought I was a goner." She shivered at the memory.

"How did you save yourself?" shrieked Katie.

"Oh I didn't. I couldn't!" explained Betty. "Just when I had lost hope, a shadow appeared above and a hand reached out to me. I was pulled up to safety." Betty pointed up to the cliff up above. "It was Mr Engel here. He saved me. He was hungry and weak with a broken arm, he was bruised and hurt, but he found the strength to save my life. He's a true hero."

"But, but, but he's a German!" shrieked Jack. "He's the enemy. He's a baddie!"

"He is a person, same as you and me," said Mr Jones. "He has a family back home and is fighting a war because it's his duty to his country. Same as our soldiers."

Betty looked at Mr Jones in surprise. "But sir, I thought you would be angry, that you wouldn't understand. You see, I had to help him, like he helped me. He was found on British soil. He would be considered a spy if caught. And you know what happens to enemy spies…"

Max and Katie looked at each other, confused. "Er, what happens to enemy spies?"

Mr Jones looked at them with a very serious expression. "They are executed."

22

The waves continued to crash to the shore.

Mr Jones had been quiet for a long time. He was clearly thinking the situation through very carefully. At long last, he started to speak.

"Yes, I understand," he said. "You feel you should repay the kindness that he showed you. But Betty, do you understand the danger to yourself, if anyone ever found out that you had chosen to help the enemy?"

Betty nodded. "I know people would say I was a spy."

Katie was horrified. "But that means, that means…"

Mr Jones looked at her. "Yes, dear Katie, I'm afraid it does. If Betty's actions were ever discovered, she could be executed as a spy." Mr Jones looked out to sea. "During the First World War, I had several friends who died. Some were captured in Europe and were executed for being spies. They weren't spies. They were just in the wrong place at the wrong time, like this chap here."

They all looked at the injured soldier.

Mr Jones shook his head. "War. It's a terrible thing. War ruins everything. It changes people. There are terrible losses on both sides. It is rarely the evil men like Hitler who suffer. It is the everyday people, like you and me. I have no doubt that this man will return to Germany and always remember and be grateful for the kindness shown to him here. He will pass that on to his children. That is how we overcome War."

Betty clapped her hands and threw her arms around Mr Jones. "So you will help him?!" she sobbed. "Thank you, oh thank you!"

23

Max wanted to clear up the mystery. "So it was you, Betty, who has been taking everything?"

"Yes," replied Betty. "I'm very sorry, Mr Jones. I took your wireless so Mr Engel could listen to secret messages transmitted by his brother. It worked too. He heard the message from his brother. They knew where the plane had crash-landed, and they said they would come to the nearest beach, our beach, this very beach!" Betty waved her hand out to sea. "We just didn't know when. I took George's glasses and his tools so Mr Engel could fix his own broken radio to try to communicate back. But that didn't work; the radio was too damaged from the crash-landing."

"Is that why you took the torch?" asked Max.

"Yes," she replied. "The torch was for Mr Engel to signal in Morse code to his brother's boat to tell him that the message was received. Then, as you know, the postcard this morning told us the time they would try their rescue. I'm so very sorry, Mr Jones, I really am. But I had to help Mr Engel get home after he saved my life."

At that moment, something caught the light out to sea. Mr Engel held the torch up and signalled with short and long flashes. Everyone held their breath. Waited. Nobody spoke.

24

Soon there was a series of flashes, then a shape appeared on the water. They strained their eyes to see in the darkness. As the shadow approached, they saw it was a small rowing boat.

The boat was almost on the beach. Jack clung to Harriet. Katie stepped closer to Max. Everyone was afraid to move. Everyone except Mr Engel, who stepped into the gentle waves and pulled the boat onto the sand. The man inside the boat jumped into the shallow water and hugged Mr Engel tightly.

They eventually let go and looked at everyone on the beach. Mr Engel reached out his hand to Betty, but she ignored that and threw her arms around his shoulders in a warm hug.

Betty then stepped away and watched in amazement as Mr Jones held out his own hand to Mr Engel. They shook hands and nodded in understanding at each other.

It was time to leave. The happy brothers pushed the boat out past the waves and jumped in. They rowed back out to sea and disappeared into the shadows.

25

Everyone made their way back up the steep steps to the farmhouse. In the kitchen, Betty busied herself and poured everyone a mug of warm milk.

Katie wanted to make sense of everything. "So if Mr Lang isn't a missing German pilot, then why doesn't he speak very much?"

Mr Jones laughed. "Well, young Katie, that is a good question. You are right in thinking Mr Lang doesn't understand much, but he is not German. He is actually from Poland. He brought his family here as refugees when the Nazis marched into his country. He is an excellent gardener, and his English will improve very quickly, I'm sure."

"So what will happen now?" asked Max.

Mr Jones smiled at Betty. "I imagine life will simply return to normal around here," he said. "But not today. Today we should have a picnic! I won't step foot in my office at all today. Let's all of us - including Mr Lang, George, Eddie and all of us here - let's go on a picnic. We should enjoy being free and safe. That is a luxury that many people across Europe and the rest of the world do not have today."

Betty, Jack, Harriet and Katie cheered. Max didn't. Instead, he held up a hand to get everyone's attention.

"We'd love to, but I'm afraid we can't join you," said Max. Katie shot him an angry look, but he continued. "Er, we got a letter from our mum today, telling us that she is coming to collect us in the village this morning." Max ignored Katie's stare and instead led her upstairs to pack their belongings.

"Spoil-sport," she hissed at him under her breath. "I was having fun!"

"But we've solved the mystery!" replied Max. "It's time to go. What if we disappear right in front of them?!"

Katie knew he was right, but she couldn't bring herself to tell him that. Instead, she packed her suitcase noisily to show how annoyed she was.

Downstairs, Betty insisted on giving them some sandwiches for their journey. They thanked her then said their goodbyes to everyone.

26

They turned and walked down the lane. Just when they were out of sight, flashes of light started to spin around them. They held hands and enjoyed the colourful ride back to modern day.

Safely back in Max's bedroom, they both sat happily against the bed.

"What will happen to Mr Jones now?" wondered Katie out loud.

"Well, he has two empty beds now. I'm sure he will take two more evacuees from the cities."

"They will be very lucky to have a happy home," replied Katie. "Come on – let's write secret notes in invisible ink."

Before Max could ask what she meant, Katie had raced halfway down the stairs. "MU-UM!" she called. "Do we have any lemons?"

The End.

See you on our next adventure.